THE MACMILLAN CLASSICS

THE FABLES OF AESOP

THE FABLES OF AESOP

SELECTED, TOLD ANEW AND
THEIR HISTORY TRACED BY
JOSEPH JACOBS

ILLUSTRATED BY DAVID LEVINE
AFTERWORD BY CLIFTON FADIMAN

THE MACMILLAN COMPANY, NEW YORK

FOURTH PRINTING, 1966

Library of Congress catalog card number: 64-21759
Printed in the United States of America

✌ *PREFACE* ✌

It is difficult to say what are and what are not the Fables of Aesop. Almost all the fables that have appeared in the Western world have been sheltered at one time or another under the shadow of that name. I could at any rate enumerate at least seven hundred which have appeared in English in various books entitled *Aesop's Fables*. L'Estrange's collection alone contains over five hundred. In the struggle for existence among all these a certain number stand out as being the most effective and the most familiar. I have attempted to bring most of these into the following pages.

There is no fixed text even for the nucleus collection contained in this book. Aesop himself is so shadowy a figure that we might almost be forgiven if we held, with regard to him, the heresy of Mistress Elizabeth Prig. What we call his fables can in most cases be traced back to the fables of other people, notably of Phaedrus and Babrius. It is usual to regard the Greek Prose Collections, passing under the name of Aesop, as having greater claims to the eponymous title; but modern research has shown that these are but medieval prosings of Babrius's verse. I have therefore felt at liberty to retell the fables in such a way as would interest children, and have adopted from the various versions that which seemed most suitable in each case, telling the fable anew in my own way.

Much has been learnt during the present century about the history of the various apologues that walk abroad under the name of "Aesop." I have attempted to bring these various lines of research together in the somewhat elaborate introductory volume which I wrote to accompany my edition of Caxton's *Æsop*, published by Mr. Nutt in his *Bibliothèque de Carabas*. I have placed in back of the present version of the "Fables," by kind permission of Mr. Nutt, the short abstract of my researches in which I there summed up the results of that volume. I must accompany it, here as there, by a warning to the reader, that for a large proportion of the results thus reached I am myself responsible; but I am happy to say that many of them have been accepted by the experts in America, France, and Germany, who have done me the honour to consider my researches. Here, in England, there does not seem to be much interest in this class of work, and English scholars, for the most part, are content to remain in ignorance of the methods and results of literary history.

JOSEPH JACOBS

✍ CONTENTS ✍

Preface	v
The Dog and the Shadow	3
The Wolf and the Lamb	4
The Man and the Serpent	6
The Mountains in Labor	7
The Lion's Share	8
The Swallow and the Other Birds	9
The Wolf and the Crane	10
The Bald Man and the Fly	11
The Town Mouse and the Country Mouse	12
The Fox and the Crow	14
The Cock and the Pearl	16
The Man and the Wood	17
The Hares and the Frogs	18
The Ass and the Lap Dog	20
The Lion and the Mouse	21
The Fox and the Mask	22
The Wolf and the Kid	23
The Frogs Desiring a King	24
The Fox and the Stork	26

The Woodman and the Serpent — 28
The Sick Lion — 29
The Bat, the Birds, and the Beasts — 30
The Serpent and the File — 31
Androcles — 32
The Jay and the Peacock — 34
The Wolf in Sheep's Clothing — 35
The Frog and the Ox — 36
The Dog and the Wolf — 38
Belling the Cat — 39
The Hart in the Ox Stall — 40
The Belly and the Members — 41
The Hart and the Hunter — 42
The Peacock and Juno — 44
The Two Crabs — 45
The Fox and the Lion — 46
The Dog in the Manger — 47
The Horse, Hunter, and Stag — 48
The Lion and the Statue — 50
The Fox and the Grapes — 51
The Ant and the Grasshopper — 52
The Lion in Love — 53
The Miser and His Gold — 54
The Tree and the Reed — 55
The Fox and the Cat — 56
The Two Pots — 58
The Fisher — 59
The Young Thief and His Mother — 60
The Two Fellows and the Bear — 61
The Shepherd's Boy — 62
The Man and the Satyr — 63
The Man and His Two Wives — 64
Avaricious and Envious — 66

The Nurse and the Wolf   67
The Tortoise and the Birds   68
The Goose with the Golden Eggs   69
The Fox, the Cock, and the Dog   70
The Man and the Wooden God   71
The Old Man and Death   72
The Ass in the Lion's Skin   73
The Four Oxen and the Lion   74
The Fisher and the Little Fish   75
The Ass's Brains   76
The Crow and the Pitcher   77
The Hare and the Tortoise   79
The Buffoon and the Countryman   80
The Laborer and the Nightingale   81
The Man, the Boy, and the Donkey   82
The Milkmaid and Her Pail   84
The One-Eyed Doe   86
The Bundle of Sticks   87
The Fox and the Mosquitoes   88
The Cat-Maiden   89
The Fox and the Goat   90
The Wind and the Sun   91
The Trumpeter Taken Prisoner   92
The Eagle and the Arrow   94
The Old Woman and the Wine Jar   95
The Fox Without a Tail   96
The Lion, the Fox, and the Beasts   97
Hercules and the Wagoner   98
The Horse and the Ass   99
The Hare with Many Friends   100

A Short History of the Aesopic Fable   104
An Afterword by Clifton Fadiman   111

THE FABLES OF AESOP

THE DOG AND
THE SHADOW

IT happened that a Dog had got a piece of meat and was carrying it home in his mouth to eat it in peace. Now on his way home he had to cross a plank lying across a running brook. As he crossed, he looked down and saw his own shadow reflected in the water beneath. Thinking it was another dog with another piece of meat, he made up his mind to have that also. So he made a snap at the shadow in the water, but as he opened his mouth the piece of meat fell out, dropped into the water and was never seen more.

Beware lest you lose the substance
by grasping at the shadow.

THE WOLF AND
THE LAMB

NCE upon a time a Wolf was lapping at a spring on a hillside, when, looking up, what should he see but a Lamb just beginning to drink a little lower down. "There's my supper," thought he, "if only I can find some excuse to seize it." Then he called out to the Lamb, "How dare you muddle the water from which I am drinking?"

"Nay, Master, nay," said Lambikin; "if the water be muddy up there, I cannot be the cause of it, for it runs down from you to me.

"Well, then," said the Wolf, "why did you call me bad names this time last year?"

"That cannot be," said the Lamb; "I am only six months old."

"I don't care," snarled the Wolf; "if it was not you, it was your father"; and with that he rushed upon the poor little Lamb and—

WARRA WARRA WARRA WARRA WARRA—

ate her all up. But before she died she gasped out—

"Any excuse will serve a tyrant."

THE MAN AND THE SERPENT

A COUNTRYMAN'S son by accident trod upon a Serpent's tail, which turned and bit him so that he died. The father in a rage got his ax, and pursuing the Serpent, cut off part of its tail. So the Serpent in revenge began stinging several of the Farmer's cattle and caused him severe loss. Well, the Farmer thought it best to make it up with the Serpent, and brought food and honey to the mouth of its lair, and said to it: "Let's forget and forgive; perhaps you were right to punish my son, and take vengeance on my cattle, but surely I was right in trying to revenge him; now that we are both satisfied why should not we be friends again?"

"No, no," said the Serpent; "take away your gifts; you can never forget the death of your son, nor I the loss of my tail."

Injuries may be forgiven, but not forgotten.

THE MOUNTAINS
IN LABOR

NE day the Countrymen noticed that the Mountains were in labor; smoke came out of their summits, the earth was quaking at their feet, trees were crashing, and huge rocks were tumbling. They felt sure that something horrible was going to happen. They all gathered together in one place to see what terrible thing this would be. They waited and they waited, but nothing came. At last there was a still more violent earthquake, and a huge gap appeared in the side of the Mountains. They all fell down upon their knees and waited. At last, and at last, a teeny, tiny mouse poked its little head and bristles out of the gap and came running down towards them; and ever after they used to say:

"Much outcry, little outcome."

THE LION'S SHARE

HE Lion went once a-hunting along with the Fox, the Jackal, and the Wolf. They hunted and they hunted till at last they surprised a Stag, and soon took its life. Then came the question how the spoil should be divided. "Quarter me this Stag," roared the Lion; so the other animals skinned it and cut it into four parts. Then the Lion took his stand in front of the carcass and pronounced judgment: "The first quarter is for me in my capacity as King of Beasts; the second is mine as arbiter; another share comes to me for my part in the chase; and as for the fourth quarter, well, as for that, I should like to see which of you will dare to lay a paw upon it."

"Humph," grumbled the Fox as he walked away with his tail between his legs; but he spoke in a low growl—

"You may share the labors of the great,
but you will not share the spoil."

THE SWALLOW AND THE OTHER BIRDS

IT happened that a Countryman was sowing some hemp seeds in a field where a Swallow and some other birds were hopping about picking up their food. "Beware of that man," quoth the Swallow.

"Why, what is he doing?" said the others.

"That is hemp seed he is sowing; be careful to pick up every one of the seeds, or else you will repent it."

The birds paid no heed to the Swallow's words, and by and by the hemp grew up and was made into cord, and of the cords nets were made, and many a bird that had despised the Swallow's advice was caught in nets made out of that very hemp. "What did I tell you?" said the Swallow.

"Destroy the seed of evil,
or it will grow up to your ruin."

THE WOLF AND
THE CRANE

WOLF had been gorging on an animal he had killed, when suddenly a small bone in the meat stuck in his throat and he could not swallow it. He soon felt terrible pain in his throat, and ran up and down groaning and groaning and seeking for something to relieve the pain. He tried to induce everyone he met to remove the bone. "I would give anything," said he, "if you would take it out." At last the Crane agreed to try, and told the Wolf to lie on his side and open his jaws as wide as he could. Then the Crane put its long neck down the Wolf's throat, and with its beak loosened the bone, till at last it got it out.

"Will you kindly give me the reward you promised?" said the Crane.

The Wolf grinned and showed his teeth and said: "Be content. You have put your head inside a Wolf's mouth and taken it out again in safety; that ought to be reward enough for you."

Gratitude and greed go not together.

THE BALD MAN
AND THE FLY

HERE was once a Bald Man who sat down after work on a hot summer's day. A Fly came up and kept buzzing about his bald pate, and stinging him from time to time. The Man aimed a blow at his little enemy, but—*whack*—his palm came on his head instead; again the Fly tormented him, but this time the Man was wiser and said:

"You will only injure yourself if you take notice of despicable enemies."

THE TOWN MOUSE AND THE COUNTRY MOUSE

NOW you must know that a Town Mouse once upon a time went on a visit to his cousin in the country. He was rough and ready, this cousin, but he loved his town friend and made him heartily welcome. Beans and bacon, cheese and bread were all he had to offer, but he offered them freely. The Town Mouse rather turned up his long nose at this country fare, and said: "I cannot understand, Cousin, how you can put up with such poor food as this, but of course you cannot expect anything better in the country; come you with me and I will show you how to live. When you have been in town a week you will wonder how you could ever have stood a country life."

No sooner said than done: the two mice set off for the town and arrived at the Town Mouse's residence late at night. "You will want some refreshment after our long journey," said the polite Town

Mouse, and took his friend into the grand dining room. There they found the remains of a fine feast, and soon the two mice were eating up jellies and cakes and all that was nice. Suddenly they heard growling and barking.

"What is that?" said the Country Mouse.

"It is only the dogs of the house," answered the other.

"Only!" said the Country Mouse. "I do not like that music at my dinner."

Just at that moment the door flew open, in came two huge mastiffs, and the two mice had to scamper down and run off.

"Good-by, Cousin," said the Country Mouse.

"What! going so soon?" said the other.

"Yes," he replied;

"Better beans and bacon in peace
than cakes and ale in fear."

THE FOX AND
THE CROW

A FOX once saw a Crow fly off with a piece of cheese in its beak and settle on a branch of a tree. "That's for me, as I am a Fox," said Master Reynard, and he walked up to the foot of the tree.

"Good day, Mistress Crow," he cried. "How well you are looking today: how glossy your feathers; how bright your eye. I feel sure your voice must surpass that of other birds, just as your figure does; let me hear but one song from you that I may greet you as the Queen of Birds."

The Crow lifted up her head and began to caw her best, but the moment she opened her mouth the piece of cheese fell to the ground, only to be snapped up by Master Fox. "That will do," said he. "That was all I wanted. In exchange for your cheese I will give you a piece of advice for the future—

Do not trust flatterers."

THE COCK AND
THE PEARL

A COCK was once strutting up and down the farmyard among the hens when suddenly he espied something shining amid the straw. "Ho! ho!" quoth he, "that's for me," and soon rooted it out from beneath the straw. What did it turn out to be but a Pearl that by some chance had been lost in the yard. "You may be a treasure," quoth Master Cock, "to men that prize you, but for me I would rather have a single barleycorn than a peck of pearls."

Precious things are for those
that can prize them.

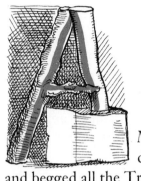

THE MAN AND
THE WOOD

MAN came into a Wood one day with an ax in his hand, and begged all the Trees to give him a small branch which he wanted for a particular purpose. The Trees were good-natured and gave him one of their branches. What did the Man do but fix it into the ax head, and soon set to work cutting down tree after tree. Then the Trees saw how foolish they had been in giving their enemy the means of destroying themselves.

THE HARES AND
THE FROGS

HE Hares were so persecuted by the other beasts, they did not know where to go. As soon as they saw a single animal approach them, off they used to run. One day they saw a troop of wild Horses stampeding about, and in quite a panic all the Hares scuttled off to a lake hard by, determined to drown themselves rather than live in such a continual state of fear. But just as they got near the bank of the lake, a troop of Frogs, frightened in their turn by the approach of the Hares, scuttled off, and jumped into the water. "Truly," said one of the Hares, "things are not so bad as they seem:

There is always some one worse off than yourself."

THE ASS AND
THE LAP DOG

FARMER one day came to the stables to see to his beasts of burden: among them was his favorite Ass, that was always well fed and often carried his master. With the Farmer came his Lap Dog, who danced about and licked his hand and frisked about as happy as could be. The Farmer felt in his pocket, gave the Lap Dog some dainty food, and sat down while he gave his orders to his servants. The Lap Dog jumped into his master's lap, and lay there blinking while the Farmer stroked his ears. The Ass, seeing this, broke loose from his halter and commenced prancing about in imitation of the Lap Dog. The Farmer could not hold his sides with laughter, so the Ass went up to him, and putting his feet upon the Farmer's shoulder attempted to climb into his lap. The Farmer's servants rushed up with sticks and pitchforks and soon taught the Ass that

Clumsy jesting is no joke.

THE LION AND
THE MOUSE

NCE when a Lion was asleep a little Mouse began running up and down upon him; this soon wakened the Lion, who placed his huge paw upon him, and opened his big jaws to swallow him. "Pardon, O King," cried the little Mouse; "forgive me this time, I shall never forget it: who knows but what I may be able to do you a turn some of these days?" The Lion was so tickled at the idea of the Mouse being able to help him, that he lifted up his paw and let him go.

Some time after, the Lion was caught in a trap, and the hunters, who desired to carry him alive to the King, tied him to a tree while they went in search of a wagon to carry him on. Just then the little Mouse happened to pass by, and seeing the sad plight in which the Lion was, went up to him and soon gnawed away the ropes that bound the King of the Beasts. "Was I not right?" said the little Mouse.

Little friends may prove great friends.

THE FOX AND
THE MASK

FOX had by some means got into the storeroom of a theater. Suddenly he observed a face glaring down on him, and began to be very frightened; but looking more closely he found it was only a Mask, such as actors use to put over their face. "Ah," said the Fox, "you look very fine; it is a pity you have not got any brains."

Outside show is a poor substitute for inner worth.

THE WOLF AND
THE KID

A KID was perched up on the top of a house, and looking down saw a Wolf passing under him. Immediately he began to revile and attack his enemy. "Murderer and thief," he cried, "what do you here near honest folks' houses? How dare you make an appearance where your vile deeds are known?"

"Curse away, my young friend," said the Wolf.

"It is easy to be brave from a safe distance."

THE FROGS DESIRING A KING

HE Frogs were living as happy as could be in a marshy swamp that just suited them; they went splashing about caring for nobody and nobody troubling with them. But some of them thought that this was not right, that they should have a king and a proper constitution, so they determined to send up a petition to Jove to give them what they wanted. "Mighty Jove," they cried, "send unto us a king that will rule over us and keep us in order." Jove laughed at their croaking, and threw down into the swamp a huge Log, which came down—*kerplash*—into the swamp. The Frogs were frightened out of their lives by the commotion made in their midst, and all rushed to the bank to look at the horrible monster; but after a time, seeing that it did not move, one or two of the boldest of them ventured out towards the Log, and even dared to touch it; still it did not move. Then the greatest hero of the Frogs jumped upon the Log and commenced dancing up and down upon it; thereupon all the Frogs came and did the same, and for some time the Frogs went about their business every day without taking the slightest notice of their new King Log lying in their midst.

But this did not suit them, so they sent another petition to Jove, and said to him: "We want a real king; one that will really rule over us." Now this made Jove angry, so he sent among them a big Stork that soon set to work gobbling them all up. Then the Frogs repented when too late.

Better no rule than cruel rule.

THE FOX AND
THE STORK

AT one time the Fox and the Stork were on visiting terms and seemed very good friends. So the Fox invited the Stork to dinner, and for a joke put nothing before her but some soup in a very shallow dish. This the Fox could easily lap up, but the Stork could only wet the end of her long bill in it, and left the meal as hungry as when she began. "I am sorry," said the Fox, "the soup is not to your liking."

"Pray do not apologize," said the Stork. "I hope you will return this visit, and come and dine with me soon." So a day was appointed when the Fox should visit the Stork; but when they were seated at table all that was for their dinner was contained in a very long-necked jar with a narrow mouth, in which the Fox could not insert his snout—so all he could manage to do was to lick the outside of the jar. "I will not apologize for the dinner," said the Stork:

"One bad turn deserves another."

27.

THE WOODMAN
AND
THE SERPENT

ONE wintry day a Woodman was tramping home from his work when he saw something black lying on the snow. When he came closer, he saw it was a Serpent, to all appearance dead. But he took it up and put it in his bosom to warm while he hurried home. As soon as he got indoors he put the Serpent down on the hearth before the fire. The children watched it and saw it slowly come to life again. Then one of them stooped down to stroke it, but the Serpent raised its head and put out its fangs and was about to sting the child to death. So the Woodman seized his ax, and with one stroke cut the Serpent in two. "Ah," said he,

"No gratitude from the wicked."

THE SICK LION

A LION had come to the end of his days and lay sick unto death at the mouth of his cave, gasping for breath. The animals, his subjects, came round him and drew nearer as he grew more and more helpless. When they saw him on the point of death they thought to themselves: "Now is the time to pay off old grudges." So the Boar came up and drove at him with his tusks; then a Bull gored him with his horns; still the Lion lay helpless before them: so the Ass, feeling quite safe from danger, came up, and turning his tail to the old Lion kicked up his heels into his face. "This is a double death," growled the Lion.

"Only cowards insult dying Majesty."

THE BAT,
THE BIRDS, AND
THE BEASTS

GREAT conflict was about to come off between the Birds and the Beasts. When the two armies were collected together the Bat hesitated which to join. The Birds that passed his perch said: "Come with us"; but he said: "I am a Beast." Later on, some Beasts who were passing underneath him looked up and said: "Come with us"; but he said: "I am a Bird." Luckily at the last moment peace was made, and no battle took place, so the Bat came to the Birds and wished to join in the rejoicings, but they all turned against him and he had to fly away. He then went to the Beasts, but had soon to beat a retreat, or else they would have torn him to pieces. "Ah," said the Bat, "I see now—

He that is neither one thing nor
the other has no friends."

THE SERPENT AND
THE FILE

A SERPENT in the course of his wanderings came into an armorer's shop. As he glided over the floor he felt his skin pricked by a file lying there. In a rage he turned round upon it and tried to dart his fangs into it; but he could do no harm to heavy iron and had soon to give over his wrath.

It is useless attacking the insensible.

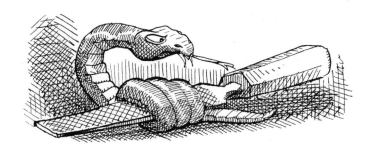

ANDROCLES

SLAVE named Androcles once escaped from his master and fled to the forest. As he was wandering about there he came upon a Lion lying down moaning and groaning. At first he turned to flee, but finding that the Lion did not pursue him, he turned back and went up to him. As he came near, the Lion put out his paw, which was all swollen and bleeding, and Androcles found that a huge thorn had got into it, and was causing all the pain. He pulled out the thorn and bound up the paw of the Lion, who was soon able to rise and lick the hand of Androcles like a dog. Then the Lion took Androcles to his cave, and every day used to bring him meat from which to live.

But shortly afterwards both Androcles and the

Lion were captured, and the slave was sentenced to be thrown to the Lion, after the latter had been kept without food for several days. The Emperor and all his Court came to see the spectacle, and Androcles was led out into the middle of the arena. Soon the Lion was let loose from his den, and rushed bounding and roaring towards his victim. But as soon as he came near to Androcles he recognized his friend, and fawned upon him, and licked his hands like a friendly dog. The Emperor, surprised at this, summoned Androcles to him, who told him the whole story. Whereupon the slave was pardoned and freed, and the Lion let loose to his native forest.

Gratitude is the sign of noble souls.

THE JAY AND
THE PEACOCK

A JAY venturing into a yard where Peacocks used to walk, found there a number of feathers which had fallen from the Peacocks when they were molting. He tied them all to his tail and strutted down towards the Peacocks. When he came near them they soon discovered the cheat, and striding up to him pecked at him and plucked away his borrowed plumes. So the Jay could do no better than go back to the other Jays, who had watched his behavior from a distance; but they were equally annoyed with him, and told him:

"It is not only fine feathers that make fine birds."

THE WOLF IN SHEEP'S CLOTHING

WOLF found great difficulty in getting at the sheep owing to the vigilance of the shepherd and his dogs. But one day it found the skin of a sheep that had been flayed and thrown aside, so it put it on over its own pelt and strolled down among the sheep. The Lamb that belonged to the sheep whose skin the Wolf was wearing began to follow the Wolf in the sheep's clothing; so, leading the Lamb a little apart, he soon made a meal off her, and for some time he succeeded in deceiving the sheep and enjoying hearty meals.

Appearances are deceptive.

THE FROG AND
THE OX

"H Father," said a little Frog to the big one sitting by the side of a pool, "I have seen such a terrible monster! It was as big as a mountain, with horns on its head, and a long tail, and it had hoofs divided in two."

"Tush, child, tush," said the old Frog, "that was only Farmer White's Ox. It isn't so big either; he may be a little bit taller than I, but I could easily make myself quite as broad; just you see." So he blew himself out, and blew himself out, and blew himself out. "Was he as big as that?" asked he.

"Oh, much bigger than that," said the young Frog.

Again the old one blew himself out, and asked the young one if the Ox was as big as that.

"Bigger, Father, bigger," was the reply.

So the Frog took a deep breath, and blew and blew and blew, and swelled and swelled and swelled. And then he said: "I'm sure the Ox is not as big as—" But at this moment he burst.

Self-conceit may lead to self-destruction.

THE DOG AND
THE WOLF

GAUNT Wolf was almost dead with hunger when he happened to meet a House Dog who was passing by. "Ah, Cousin," said the Dog, "I knew how it would be; your irregular life will soon be the ruin of you. Why do you not work steadily as I do, and get your food regularly given to you?"

"I would have no objection," said the Wolf, "if I could only get a place."

"I will easily arrange that for you," said the Dog; "come with me to my master and you shall share my work."

So the Wolf and the Dog went towards the town together. On the way there the Wolf noticed that the hair on a certain part of the Dog's neck was very much worn away, so he asked him how that had come about.

"Oh, it is nothing," said the Dog. "That is only the place where the collar is put on at night to keep me chained up; it chafes a bit, but one soon gets used to it."

"It that all?" said the Wolf. "Then goodby to you, Master Dog.

"Better starve free than be a fat slave."

BELLING
THE CAT

LONG ago, the mice held a general council to consider what measures they could take to outwit their common enemy, the Cat. Some said this, and some said that; but at last a young mouse got up and said he had a proposal to make, which he thought would meet the case. "You will all agree," said he, "that our chief danger consists in the sly and treacherous manner in which the enemy approaches us. Now, if we could receive some signal of her approach, we could easily escape from her. I venture, therefore, to propose that a small bell be procured, and attached by a ribbon round the neck of the Cat. By this means we should always know when she was about, and could easily retire while she was in the neighborhood."

This proposal met with general applause, until an old mouse got up and said: "That is all very well, but who is to bell the Cat?" The mice looked at one another, and nobody spoke. Then the old mouse said:

"It is easy to propose impossible remedies."

THE HART IN
THE OX STALL

A HART hotly pursued by the hounds fled for refuge into an ox stall, and buried itself in a truss of hay, leaving nothing to be seen but the tips of his horns. Soon after, the Hunters came up and asked if anyone had seen the Hart. The stable boys, who had been resting after their dinner, looked round, but could see nothing, and the Hunters went away. Shortly afterwards the master came in, and, looking round, saw that something unusual had taken place. He pointed to the truss of hay and said: "What are those two curious things sticking out of the hay?" And when the stable boys came to look they discovered the Hart, and soon made an end of him. He thus learnt that

Nothing escapes the master's eye.

THE BELLY AND
THE MEMBERS

NE fine day it occurred to the Members of the Body that they were doing all the work and the Belly was having all the food. So they held a meeting, and after a long discussion decided to strike work till the Belly consented to take its proper share of the work. So for a day or two the Hands refused to take the food, the Mouth refused to receive it, and the Teeth had no work to do. But after a day or two the Members began to find that they themselves were not in a very active condition: the Hands could hardly move, and the Mouth was all parched and dry, while the Legs were unable to support the rest. So thus they found that even the Belly in its dull quiet way was doing necessary work for the Body, and that all must work together or the Body will go to pieces.

THE HART AND
THE HUNTER

THE Hart was once drinking from a pool and admiring the noble figure he made there. "Ah," said he, "where can you see such noble horns as these, with such antlers! I wish I had legs more worthy to bear such a noble crown; it is a pity they are so slim and slight." At that moment a Hunter approached and sent an arrow whistling after him. Away bounded the Hart, and soon, by the aid of his nimble legs, was nearly out of sight of the Hunter; but not noticing where he was going, he passed under some trees with branches growing low down in which his antlers were caught, so that the Hunter had time to come up. "Alas! alas!" cried the Hart:

"We often despise what is most useful to us."

THE PEACOCK
AND JUNO

PEACOCK once placed a petition before Juno desiring to have the voice of a nightingale in addition to his other attractions; but Juno refused his request. When he persisted, and pointed out that he was her favorite bird, she said:

*"Be content with your lot;
one cannot be first in everything."*

THE TWO CRABS

ONE fine day two Crabs came out from their home to take a stroll on the sand. "Child," said the mother, "you are walking very ungracefully. You should accustom yourself to walking straight forward without twisting from side to side."

"Pray, Mother," said the young one, "do but set the example yourself, and I will follow you."

Example is the best precept.

THE FOX AND
THE LION

WHEN first the Fox saw the Lion he was terribly frightened, and ran away and hid himself in the wood. Next time, however, he came near the King of Beasts he stopped at a safe distance and watched him pass by. The third time they came near one another the Fox went straight up to the Lion and passed the time of day with him, asking him how his family were, and when he should have the pleasure of seeing him again; then turning his tail, he parted from the Lion without much ceremony.

Familiarity breeds contempt.

THE DOG IN
THE MANGER

A DOG looking out for its afternoon nap jumped into the Manger of an Ox and lay there cozily upon the straw. But soon the Ox, returning from its afternoon work, came up to the Manger and wanted to eat some of the straw. The Dog in a rage, being awakened from its slumber, stood up and barked at the Ox, and whenever it came near attempted to bite it. At last the Ox had to give up the hope of getting at the straw, and went away muttering:

"Ah, people often grudge others
what they cannot enjoy themselves."

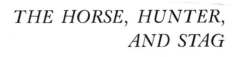

THE HORSE, HUNTER, AND STAG

QUARREL had arisen between the Horse and the Stag, so the Horse came to a Hunter to ask his help to take revenge on the Stag. The Hunter agreed, but said: "If you desire to conquer the Stag, you must permit me to place this piece of iron between your jaws, so that I may guide you with these reins, and allow this saddle to be placed upon your back so that I may keep steady upon you as we follow after the enemy." The Horse agreed to the conditions, and the Hunter soon saddled and bridled him. Then with the aid of the Hunter the Horse soon overcame the Stag, and said to the Hunter: "Now, get off, and remove those things from my mouth and back."

"Not so fast, friend," said the Hunter. "I have now got you under bit and spur, and prefer to keep you as you are at present."

If you allow men to use you for your own purposes, they will use you for theirs.

THE LION AND THE STATUE

MAN and a Lion were discussing the relative strength of men and lions in general. The Man contended that he and his fellows were stronger than lions by reason of their greater intelligence. "Come now with me," he cried, "and I will soon prove that I am right." So he took him into the public gardens and showed him a statue of Hercules overcoming the Lion and tearing his mouth in two.

"That is all very well," said the Lion, "but proves nothing, for it was a man who made the statue."

We can easily represent things
as we wish them to be.

THE FOX AND
THE GRAPES

NE hot summer's day a Fox was strolling through an orchard till he came to a bunch of Grapes just ripening on a vine which had been trained over a lofty branch. "Just the thing to quench my thirst," quoth he. Drawing back a few paces, he took a run and a jump, and just missed the bunch. Turning round again with a One, Two, Three, he jumped up, but with no greater success. Again and again he tried after the tempting morsel, but at last had to give it up, and walked away with his nose in the air, saying: "I am sure they are sour."

It is easy to despise what you cannot get.

THE ANT AND
THE GRASSHOPPER

IN a field one summer's day a Grasshopper was hopping about, chirping and singing to its heart's content. An Ant passed by, bearing along with great toil an ear of corn he was taking to the nest.

"Why not come and chat with me," said the Grasshopper, "instead of toiling and moiling in that way?"

"I am helping to lay up food for the winter," said the Ant, "and recommend you to do the same."

"Why bother about winter?" said the Grasshopper; "we have got plenty of food at present." But the Ant went on its way and continued its toil. When the winter came the Grasshopper had no food, and found itself dying of hunger, while it saw the ants distributing every day corn and grain from the stores they had collected in the summer. Then the Grasshopper knew

It is best to prepare for the days of necessity.

THE LION
IN LOVE

A LION once fell in love with a beautiful maiden and proposed marriage to her parents. The old people did not know what to say. They did not like to give their daughter to the Lion, yet they did not wish to enrage the King of Beasts. At last the father said: "We feel highly honored by Your Majesty's proposal, but you see our daughter is a tender young thing, and we fear that in the vehemence of your affection you might possibly do her some injury. Might I venture to suggest that Your Majesty should have your claws removed, and your teeth extracted, then we would gladly consider your proposal again." The Lion was so much in love that he had his claws trimmed and his big teeth taken out. But when he came again to the parents of the young girl they simply laughed in his face, and bade him do his worst.

Love can tame the wildest.

THE MISER AND
HIS GOLD

NCE upon a time there was a Miser who used to hide his gold at the foot of a tree in his garden; but every week he used to go and dig it up and gloat over his gains. A robber, who had noticed this, went and dug up the gold and decamped with it. When the Miser next came to gloat over his treasures, he found nothing but the empty hole. He tore his hair, and raised such an outcry that all the neighbors came around him, and he told them how he used to come and visit his gold. "Did you ever take any of it out?" asked one of them.

"Nay," said he, "I only came to look at it."

"Then come again and look at the hole," said a neighbor; "it will do you just as much good."

Wealth unused might as well not exist.

THE TREE AND
THE REED

WELL, little one," said a Tree to a
Reed that was growing at its foot,
"why do you not plant your feet deeply in the
ground, and raise your head boldly in the air as I
do?"

"I am contented with my lot," said the Reed.
"I may not be so grand, but I think I am safer."

"Safe!" sneered the Tree. "Who shall pluck me
up by the roots or bow my head to the ground?"
But it soon had to repent of its boasting, for a
hurricane arose which tore it up from its roots,
and cast it a useless log on the ground, while the
little Reed, bending to the force of the wind, soon
stood upright again when the storm had passed
over.

Obscurity often brings safety.

THE FOX AND
THE CAT

FOX was boasting to a Cat of its clever devices for escaping its enemies. "I have a whole bag of tricks," he said, "which contains a hundred ways of escaping my enemies."

"I have only one," said the Cat; "but I can generally manage with that." Just at that moment they heard the cry of a pack of hounds coming towards them, and the Cat immediately scampered up a tree and hid herself in the boughs. "This is my plan," said the Cat. "What are you going to do?" The Fox thought first of one way, then of another, and while he was debating the hounds came nearer and nearer, and at last the Fox in his confusion was caught up by the hounds and soon killed by the huntsmen.

Miss Puss, who had been looking on, said:

"*Better one safe way than a hundred
on which you cannot reckon.*"

THE TWO POTS

TWO Pots had been left on the bank of a river, one of brass, and one of earthenware. When the tide rose they both floated off down the stream. Now the earthenware pot tried its best to keep aloof from the brass one, which cried out: "Fear nothing, friend, I will not strike you."

"But I may come in contact with you," said the other, "if I come too close; and whether I hit you, or you hit me, I shall suffer for it."

The strong and the weak cannot keep company.

THE FISHER

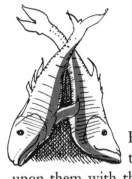

A FISHER once took his bagpipes to the bank of a river, and played upon them with the hope of making the fish rise; but never a one put his nose out of the water. So he cast his net into the river and soon drew it forth filled with fish. Then he took his bagpipes again, and, as he played, the fish leapt up in the net. "Ah, you dance now when I play," said he.

"Yes," said an old Fish:

*"When you are in a man's power
you must do as he bids you."*

THE YOUNG THIEF
AND HIS MOTHER

 YOUNG man had been caught in a daring act of theft and had been condemned to be executed for it. He expressed his desire to see his Mother, and to speak with her before he was led to execution, and of course this was granted. When his Mother came to him he said: "I want to whisper to you," and when she brought her ear near him, he nearly bit it off. All the bystanders were horrified, and asked him what he could mean by such brutal and inhuman conduct. "It is to punish her," he said. "When I was young I began with stealing little things, and brought them home to Mother. Instead of rebuking and punishing me, she laughed and said: 'It will not be noticed.' It is because of her that I am here today."

"He is right, woman," said the Priest; "the Lord hath said:

'Train up a child in the way he should go; and when he is old he will not depart therefrom.'"

THE TWO FELLOWS
AND THE BEAR

WO Fellows were traveling together through a wood, when a Bear rushed out upon them. One of the travelers happened to be in front, and he seized hold of the branch of a tree, and hid himself among the leaves. The other, seeing no help for it, threw himself flat down upon the ground, with his face in the dust. The Bear, coming up to him, put his muzzle close to his ear, and sniffed and sniffed. But at last with a growl he shook his head and slouched off, for bears will not touch dead meat. Then the fellow in the tree came down to his comrade, and, laughing, said: "What was it that Master Bruin whispered to you?"

"He told me," said the other,

"Never trust a friend who deserts you at a pinch."

THE SHEPHERD'S BOY

HERE was once a young Shepherd Boy who tended his sheep at the foot of a mountain near a dark forest. It was rather lonely for him all day, so he thought upon a plan by which he could get a little company and some excitement. He rushed down towards the village calling out "Wolf, Wolf," and the villagers came out to meet him, and some of them stopped with him for a considerable time. This pleased the boy so much that a few days afterwards he tried the same trick, and again the villagers came to his help. But shortly after this a Wolf actually did come out from the forest, and began to worry the sheep, and the boy of course cried out "Wolf, Wolf," still louder than before. But this time the villagers, who had been fooled twice before, thought the boy was again deceiving them, and nobody stirred to come to his help. So the Wolf made a good meal off the boy's flock, and when the boy complained, the wise man of the village said:

"A liar will not be believed,
even when he speaks the truth."

THE MAN AND
THE SATYR

MAN had lost his way in a wood one bitter winter's night. As he was roaming about, a Satyr came up to him, and finding that he had lost his way, promised to give him a lodging for the night, and guide him out of the forest in the morning. As he went along to the Satyr's cell, the Man raised both his hands to his mouth and kept on blowing at them. "What do you do that for?" said the Satyr.

"My hands are numb with the cold," said the Man, "and my breath warms them."

After this they arrived at the Satyr's home, and soon the Satyr put a smoking dish of porridge before him. But when the Man raised his spoon to his mouth he began blowing upon it. "And what do you do that for?" said the Satyr.

"The porridge is too hot, and my breath will cool it."

"Out you go," said the Satyr. "I will have nought to do with a man who can blow hot and cold with the same breath."

THE MAN AND
HIS TWO WIVES

IN the old days, when men were allowed to have many wives, a middle-aged Man had one wife that was old and one that was young; each loved him very much, and desired to see him like herself. Now the Man's hair was turning gray, which the young Wife did not like, as it made him look too old for her husband. So every night she used to comb his hair and pick out the white ones. But the elder Wife saw her husband growing gray with great pleasure, for she did not like to be mistaken for his mother. So every morning she used to arrange his hair and pick out as many of the black ones as she could. The consequence was the Man soon found himself entirely bald.

Yield to all and you will soon have nothing to yield.

AVARICIOUS AND ENVIOUS

TWO neighbors came before Jupiter and prayed him to grant their hearts' desire. Now the one was full of avarice, and the other eaten up with envy. So to punish them both, Jupiter granted that each might have whatever he wished for himself, but only on condition that his neighbor had twice as much. The Avaricious Man prayed to have a room full of gold. No sooner said than done; but all his joy was turned to grief when he found that his neighbor had two rooms full of the precious metal. Then came the turn of the Envious Man, who could not bear to think that his neighbor had any joy at all. So he prayed that he might have one of his own eyes put out, by which means his companion would become totally blind.

Vices are their own punishment.

THE NURSE AND
THE WOLF

E quiet now," said an old Nurse to a child sitting on her lap. "If you make that noise again I will throw you to the Wolf."

Now it chanced that a Wolf was passing close under the window as this was said. So he crouched down by the side of the house and waited. "I am in good luck today," thought he. "It is sure to cry soon, and a daintier morsel I haven't had for many a long day." So he waited, and he waited, and he waited, till at last the child began to cry, and the Wolf came forward before the window, and looked up to the Nurse, wagging his tail. But all the Nurse did was to shut down the window and call for help, and the dogs of the house came rushing out. "Ah," said the Wolf as he galloped away,

"Enemies' promises were made to be broken."

THE TORTOISE
AND
THE BIRDS

A TORTOISE desired to change its place of residence, so he asked an Eagle to carry him to his new home, promising her a rich reward for her trouble. The Eagle agreed and, seizing the Tortoise by the shell with her talons, soared aloft. On their way they met a Crow, who said to the Eagle: "Tortoise is good eating."

"The shell is too hard," said the Eagle in reply.

"The rocks will soon crack the shell," was the Crow's answer; and the Eagle, taking the hint, let fall the Tortoise on a sharp rock, and the two birds made a hearty meal off the Tortoise.

Never soar aloft on an enemy's pinions.

THE GOOSE
WITH THE
GOLDEN EGGS

NE day a countryman going to the nest of his Goose found there an egg all yellow and glittering. When he took it up it was as heavy as lead, and he was going to throw it away because he thought a trick had been played upon him. But he took it home on second thoughts, and soon found to his delight that it was an egg of pure gold. Every morning the same thing occurred, and he soon became rich by selling his eggs. As he grew rich he grew greedy; and thinking to get at once all the gold the Goose could give, he killed it and opened it only to find—nothing.

Greed oft o'erreaches itself.

THE FOX,
THE COCK, AND
THE DOG

ONE moonlight night a Fox was prowling about a farmer's hencoop, and saw a cock roosting high up beyond his reach. "Good news, good news!" he cried.

"Why, what is that?" said the Cock.

"King Lion has declared a universal truce. No beast may hurt a bird henceforth, but all shall dwell together in brotherly friendship."

"Why, that is good news," said the Cock; "and there I see someone coming, with whom we can share the good tidings." And so saying he craned his neck forward and looked afar off.

"What is it you see?" said the Fox.

"It is only my master's Dog that is coming towards us. What, going so soon?" he continued, as the Fox began to turn away as soon as he had heard the news. "Will you not stop and congratulate the Dog on the reign of universal peace?"

"I would gladly do so," said the Fox, "but I fear he may not have heard of King Lion's decree."

Cunning often outwits itself.

THE MAN AND
THE WOODEN GOD

N the old days men used to worship stocks and stones and idols, and prayed to them to give them luck. It happened that a Man had often prayed to a wooden idol he had received from his father, but his luck never seemed to change. He prayed and he prayed, but still he remained as unlucky as ever. One day in the greatest rage he went to the Wooden God, and with one blow swept it down from its pedestal. The idol broke in two, and what did he see? An immense number of coins flying all over the place.

THE OLD MAN
AND DEATH

N old laborer, bent double with age and toil, was gathering sticks in a forest. At last he grew so tired and hopeless that he threw down the bundle of sticks, and cried out: "I cannot bear this life any longer. Ah, I wish Death would only come and take me!"

As he spoke, Death, a grisly skeleton, appeared and said to him: "What wouldst thou, Mortal? I heard thee call me."

"Please, sir," replied the woodcutter, "would you kindly help me to lift this fagot of sticks onto my shoulder?"

We would often be sorry
if our wishes were gratified.

THE ASS IN
THE LION'S SKIN

AN Ass once found a Lion's skin which the hunters had left out in the sun to dry. He put it on and went towards his native village. All fled at his approach, both men and animals, and he was a proud Ass that day. In his delight he lifted up his voice and brayed, but then every one knew him, and his owner came up and gave him a sound cudgeling for the fright he had caused. And shortly afterwards a Fox came up to him and said: "Ah, I knew you by your voice."

Fine clothes may disguise,
but silly words will disclose a fool.

THE FOUR OXEN
AND THE LION

LION used to prowl about a field in which Four Oxen used to dwell. Many a time he tried to attack them; but whenever he came near they turned their tails to one another, so that whichever way he approached them he was met by the horns of one of them. At last, however, they fell a-quarreling among themselves, and each went off to pasture alone in a separate corner of the field. Then the Lion attacked them one by one and soon made an end of all four.

United we stand, divided we fall.

THE FISHER AND
THE LITTLE FISH

IT happened that a Fisher, after fishing all day, caught only a little Fish. "Pray, let me go, Master," said the Fish. "I am much too small for your eating just now. If you put me back into the river I shall soon grow, then you can make a fine meal off me."

"Nay, nay, my little Fish," said the Fisher, "I have you now. I may not catch you hereafter."

A little thing in hand is worth more than a great thing in prospect.

THE
ASS'S BRAINS

HE Lion and the Fox went hunting together. The Lion, on the advice of the Fox, sent a message to the Ass, proposing to make an alliance between their two families. The Ass came to the place of meeting, overjoyed at the prospect of a royal alliance. But when he came there the Lion simply pounced on the Ass, and said to the Fox: "Here is our dinner for today. Watch you here while I go and have a nap. Woe betide you if you touch my prey." The Lion went away and the Fox waited; but finding that his master did not return, ventured to take out the brains of the Ass and ate them up. When the Lion came back he soon noticed the absence of the brains, and asked the Fox in a terrible voice: "What have you done with the brains?"

"Brains, Your Majesty! It had none, or it would never have fallen into your trap."

Wit has always an answer ready.

THE CROW AND
THE PITCHER

A CROW, half dead with thirst, came upon a Pitcher which had once been full of water; but when the Crow put its beak into the mouth of the Pitcher he found that only very little water was left in it, and that he could not reach far enough down to get at it. He tried, and he tried, but at last had to give up in despair. Then a thought came to him, and he took a pebble and dropped it into the Pitcher. Then he took another pebble and dropped it into the Pitcher. Then he took another pebble and dropped that into the Pitcher. Then he took another pebble and dropped that into the Pitcher. Then he took another pebble and dropped that into the Pitcher. Then he took another pebble and dropped that into the Pitcher. At last, at last, he saw the water mount up near him; and after casting in a few more pebbles he was able to quench his thirst and save his life.

Little by little does the trick.

THE HARE AND
THE TORTOISE

THE Hare was once boasting of his speed before the other animals. "I have never yet been beaten," said he, "when I put forth my full speed. I challenge any one here to race with me."

The Tortoise said quietly: "I accept your challenge."

"That is a good joke," said the Hare; "I could dance round you all the way."

"Keep your boasting till you've beaten," answered the Tortoise. "Shall we race?"

So a course was fixed, and a start was made. The Hare darted almost out of sight at once, but soon stopped and, to show his contempt for the Tortoise, lay down to have a nap. The Tortoise plodded on and plodded on, and when the Hare awoke from his nap, he saw the Tortoise just near the winning post and could not run up in time to save the race. Then said the Tortoise:

"Plodding wins the race."

THE BUFFOON
AND THE
COUNTRYMAN

T a country fair there was a Buffoon who made all the people laugh by imitating the cries of various animals. He finished off by squeaking so like a pig that the spectators thought that he had a porker concealed about him. But a Countryman who stood by said: "Call that a pig's squeak! Nothing like it. You give me till tomorrow and I will show you what it's like." The audience laughed, but next day, sure enough, the Countryman appeared on the stage, and putting his head down squealed so hideously that the spectators hissed and threw stones at him to make him stop. "You fools!" he cried, "see what you have been hissing," and held up a little pig whose ear he had been pinching to make him utter the squeals.

Men often applaud an imitation
and hiss the real thing.

THE LABORER
AND THE
NIGHTINGALE

A LABORER lay listening to a Nightingale's song throughout the summer night. So pleased was he with it that the next night he set a trap for it and captured it. "Now that I have caught thee," he cried, "thou shalt always sing to me."

"We Nightingales never sing in a cage," said the bird.

"Then I'll eat thee," said the Laborer. "I have always heard say that nightingale on toast is a dainty morsel."

"Nay, kill me not," said the Nightingale; "but let me free, and I'll tell thee three things far better worth than my poor body." The Laborer let him loose, and he flew up to a branch of a tree and said: "Never believe a captive's promise; that's one thing. Then again: Keep what you have. And a third piece of advice is: Sorrow not over what is lost forever." Then the songbird flew away.

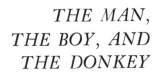

THE MAN, THE BOY, AND THE DONKEY

A MAN and his son were once going with their Donkey to market. As they were walking along by its side a countryman passed them and said: "You fools, what is a Donkey for but to ride upon?"

So the Man put the Boy on the Donkey, and they went on their way. But soon they passed a group of men, one of whom said: "See that lazy youngster, he lets his father walk while he rides."

So the Man ordered his Boy to get off, and got on himself. But they hadn't gone far when they passed two women, one of whom said to the other: "Shame on that lazy lout to let his poor little son trudge along."

Well, the Man didn't know what to do, but at at last he took his Boy up before him on the Donkey. By this time they had come to the town, and the passers-by began to jeer and point at them.

The Man stopped and asked what they were scoffing at. The men said: "Aren't you ashamed of yourself for overloading that poor Donkey of yours—you and your hulking son?"

The Man and Boy got off and tried to think what to do. They thought and they thought, till at last they cut down a pole, tied the Donkey's feet to it, and raised the pole and the Donkey to their shoulders. They went along amid the laughter of all who met them till they came to Market Bridge, when the Donkey, getting one of his feet loose, kicked out and caused the Boy to drop his end of the pole. In the struggle the Donkey fell over the bridge, and his fore-feet being tied together he was drowned.

"That will teach you," said an old man who had followed them:

"Please all, and you will please none."

THE MILKMAID
AND HER PAIL

PATTY, the Milkmaid, was going to market carrying her milk in a Pail on her head. As she went along, she began calculating what she would do with the money she would get for the milk. "I'll buy some fowls from Farmer Brown," said she, "and they will lay eggs each morning, which I will sell to the parson's wife. With the money that I get from the sale of these eggs I'll buy myself a new dimity frock and a chip hat; and when I go to market, won't all the young men come up and speak to me! Polly Shaw will be that jealous; but I don't care. I shall just look at her and toss my head like this." As she spoke, she tossed her head back, the Pail fell off it, and all the milk was spilt. So she had to go home and tell her mother what had occurred.

"Ah, my child," said her mother,

"*Do not count your chickens
before they are hatched.*"

THE
ONE–EYED DOE

A DOE had had the misfortune to lose one of her eyes, and could not see any one approaching her on that side. So to avoid any danger she always used to feed on a high cliff near the sea, with her sound eye looking towards the land. By this means she could see whenever the hunters approached her on land, and often escaped by this means. But the hunters found out that she was blind of one eye, and hiring a boat rowed under the cliff where she used to feed, and shot her from the sea. "Ah," cried she with her dying voice,

"You cannot escape your fate."

THE BUNDLE
OF STICKS

AN old man on the point of death summoned his sons around him to give them some parting advice. He ordered his servants to bring in a fagot of sticks, and said to his eldest son: "Break it." The son strained and strained, but with all his efforts was unable to break the Bundle. The other sons also tried, but none of them was successful. "Untie the fagots," said the father, "and each of you take a stick." When they had done so, he called out to them: "Now, break," and each stick was easily broken. "You see my meaning," said their father.

Union gives strength.

THE FOX AND
THE MOSQUITOES

A FOX after crossing a river got its tail entangled in a bush, and could not move. A number of Mosquitoes seeing its plight settled upon it and enjoyed a good meal undisturbed by its tail. A hedgehog strolling by took pity upon the Fox and went up to him: "You are in a bad way, neighbor," said the hedgehog; "shall I relieve you by driving off those Mosquitoes who are sucking your blood?"

"Thank you, Master Hedgehog," said the Fox, "but I would rather not."

"Why, how is that?" asked the hedgehog.

"Well, you see," was the answer, "these Mosquitoes have had their fill; if you drive these away, others will come with fresh appetite and bleed me to death."

THE
CAT–MAIDEN

THE gods were once disputing whether it was possible for a living being to change its nature. Jupiter said "Yes," but Venus said "No." So, to try the question, Jupiter turned a Cat into a Maiden, and gave her to a young man for wife. The wedding was duly performed and the young couple sat down to the wedding feast. "See," said Jupiter to Venus, "how becomingly she behaves. Who could tell that yesterday she was but a Cat? Surely her nature is changed?"

"Wait a minute," replied Venus, and let loose a mouse into the room. No sooner did the bride see this than she jumped up from her seat and tried to pounce upon the mouse. "Ah, you see," said Venus,

"Nature will out."

THE FOX AND THE GOAT

Y an unlucky chance a Fox fell into a deep well from which he could not get out. A Goat passed by shortly afterwards, and asked the Fox what he was doing down there. "Oh, have you not heard?" said the Fox; "there is going to be a great drought, so I jumped down here in order to be sure to have water by me. Why don't you come down too?" The Goat thought well of this advice, and jumped down into the well. But the Fox immediately jumped on her back, and by putting his foot on her long horns managed to jump up to the edge of the well. "Good-by, friend," said the Fox; "remember next time,

"Never trust the advice of a man in difficulties."

THE WIND AND
THE SUN

THE Wind and the Sun were disputing which was the stronger. Suddenly they saw a traveler coming down the road, and the Sun said: "I see a way to decide our dispute. Whichever of us can cause that traveler to take off his cloak shall be regarded as the stronger. You begin." So the Sun retired behind a cloud, and the Wind began to blow as hard as it could upon the traveler. But the harder he blew the more closely did the traveler wrap his cloak round him, till at last the Wind had to give up in despair. Then the Sun came out and shone in all his glory upon the traveler, who soon found it too hot to walk with his cloak on.

Kindness effects more than Severity.

THE TRUMPETER
TAKEN PRISONER

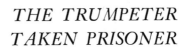

TRUMPETER during a battle ventured too near the enemy, and was captured by them. They were about to proceed to put him to death when he begged them to hear his plea for mercy. "I do not fight," said he, "and indeed carry no weapon; I only blow this trumpet, and surely that cannot harm you; then why should you kill me?"

"You may not fight yourself," said the others, "but you encourage and guide your men to the fight."

Words may be deeds.

93 .

THE EAGLE AND
THE ARROW

AN Eagle was soaring through the air when suddenly it heard the whiz of an Arrow, and felt itself wounded to death. Slowly it fluttered down to the earth, with its lifeblood pouring out of it. Looking down upon the Arrow with which it had been pierced, it found that the haft of the Arrow had been feathered with one of its own plumes. "Alas!" it cried, as it died,

"We often give our enemies
the means for our own destruction."

THE OLD
WOMAN AND
THE WINE JAR

YOU must know that sometimes old women like a glass of wine. One of this sort once found a Wine Jar lying in the road, and eagerly went up to it hoping to find it full. But when she took it up she found that all the wine had been drunk out of it. Still she took a long sniff at the mouth of the Jar. "Ah," she cried,

"What memories cling round
the instruments of our pleasure."

THE FOX WITHOUT A TAIL

T happened that a Fox caught its tail in a trap, and in struggling to release himself lost all of it but the stump. At first he was ashamed to show himself among his fellow foxes. But at last he determined to put a bolder face upon his misfortune, and summoned all the foxes to a general meeting to consider a proposal which he had to place before them. When they had assembled together the Fox proposed that they should all do away with their tails. He pointed out how inconvenient a tail was when they were pursued by their enemies, the dogs, how much it was in the way when they desired to sit down and hold a friendly conversation with one another. He failed to see any advantage in carrying about such a useless encumbrance. "That is all very well," said one of the older foxes; "but I do not think you would have recommended us to dispense with our chief ornament if you had not happened to lose it yourself."

Distrust interested advice.

THE LION,
THE FOX, AND
THE BEASTS

HE Lion once gave out that he was sick unto death, and summoned the animals to come and hear his last will and testament. So the Goat came to the Lion's cave, and stopped there listening for a long time. Then a Sheep went in, and before she came out a Calf came up to receive the last wishes of the Lord of the Beasts. But soon the Lion seemed to recover, and came to the mouth of his cave, and saw the Fox who had been waiting outside for some time. "Why do you not come to pay your respects to me?" said the Lion to the Fox.

"I beg Your Majesty's pardon," said the Fox, "but I noticed the track of the animals that have already come to you; and while I see many hoof marks going in, I see none coming out. Till the animals that have entered your cave come out again I prefer to remain in the open air."

It is easier to get into the enemy's toils than out again.

HERCULES AND
THE WAGONER

A WAGONER was once driv-
ing a heavy load along a very
muddy way. At last he came to a part of the road
where the wheels sank halfway into the mire, and
the more the horses pulled, the deeper sank the
wheels. So the Wagoner threw down his whip,
and knelt down and prayed to Hercules the Strong.
"O Hercules, help me in this my hour of distress,"
quoth he. But Hercules appeared to him, and said:

"Tut, man, don't sprawl there. Get up and put
your shoulder to the wheel."

The gods help them that help themselves.

THE HORSE
AND THE ASS

HORSE and an Ass were traveling together, the Horse prancing along in its fine trappings, the Ass carrying with difficulty the heavy weight in its panniers. "I wish I were you," sighed the Ass; "nothing to do and well fed, and all that fine harness upon you." Next day, however, there was a great battle, and the Horse was wounded to death in the final charge of the day. His friend, the Ass, happened to pass by shortly afterwards and found him on the point of death. "I was wrong," said the Ass:

"Better humble security than gilded danger."

THE HARE WITH
MANY FRIENDS

HARE was very popular with the other beasts, who all claimed to be her friends. But one day she heard the hounds approaching and hoped to escape them by the aid of her many Friends. So she went to the horse, and asked him to carry her away from the hounds on his back. But he declined, stating that he had important work to do for his master. He felt sure, he said, that all her other friends would come to her assistance. She then applied to the bull, and hoped that he would repel the hounds with his horns. The bull replied: "I am very sorry, but I have an appointment with a lady; but I feel sure that our friend the goat will do what you want." The goat, however, feared that his back might do her some harm if he took her upon it. The ram, he felt sure, was the proper friend to apply to. So she went to the ram and told him the case. The ram replied: "Another time, my dear friend. I do not like to interfere on the present occasion, as hounds have been known to eat sheep as well as hares."

The Hare then applied, as a last hope, to the calf, who regretted that he was unable to help her, as he did not like to take the responsibility upon himself, as so many older persons than himself had declined the task. By this time the hounds were quite near, and the Hare took to her heels and luckily escaped.

He that has many friends has no friends.

And this is the end of Aesop's Fables.

HURRAH!

THE END

SO the tales were told ages before Aesop; and asses under lions' manes roared in Hebrew; and sly foxes flattered in Etruscan; and wolves in sheep's clothing gnashed their teeth in Sanskrit, no doubt.

WILLIAM MAKEPEACE THACKERAY
The Newcomes

A SHORT HISTORY OF THE
∾ AESOPIC FABLE ∾

by JOSEPH JACOBS

Most nations develop the Beast-Tale as part of their
folk-lore, some go further and apply it to satiric purposes, and a few nations afford isolated examples of
the shaping of the Beast-Tale to teach some moral
truth by means of the Fable properly so called.[1] But
only two peoples independently made this a general
practice. Both in Greece [2] and in India we find in the
earliest literature such casual and frequent mention of
Fables as seems to imply a body of Folk-Fables current
among the people. And in both countries special cir-
cumstances raised the Fable from folklore into literature. In Greece, during the epoch of the Tyrants,
when free speech was dangerous, the Fable was largely
used for political purposes. The inventor of this ap-
plication or the most prominent user of it was one
Aesop, a slave at Samos whose name has ever since been
connected with the Fable. All that we know about him
is contained in a few lines of Herodotus: that he flour-
ished 550 B.C.; was killed in accordance with a Delphian
oracle; and that *wergild* was claimed for him by the

[1] *E.g.*, Jotham's Fable, Judges ix, and that of Menenius Agrippa in
Livy, seem to be quite independent of either Greek or Indian in-
fluence. But one fable does not make Fable.
[2] Only about twenty fables, however, are known in Greece before
Phaedrus, 30 A.D.

grandson of his master Iadmon. When free speech was established in the Greek democracies, the custom of using Fables in harangues was continued and encouraged by the rhetoricians, while the mirth-producing qualities of the Fable caused it to be regarded as fit subject of after-dinner conversation along with other jests of a broader kind ("Milesian," "Sybaritic"). This habit of regarding the Fable as a form of the Jest intensified the tendency to connect it with a well-known name as in the case of our Joe Miller. About 300 B.C. Demetrius Phalereus, whilom tyrant of Athens and founder of the Alexandria Library, collected together all the Fables he could find under the title of *Assemblies of Æsopic Tales* (Λόγων Αἰσωπείων συναγωγαι). This collection, running probably to some 200 Fables, after being interpolated and edited by the Alexandrine grammarians, was turned into neat Latin iambics by Phaedrus, a Greek freedman of Augustus in the early years of the Christian era. As the modern Aesop is mainly derived from Phaedrus, the answer to the question "Who wrote Aesop?" is simple. "Demetrius of Phaleron."

In India the great ethical reformer, Sakyamuni, the Buddha, initiated (or adopted from the Brahmins) the habit of using the Beast-Tale for moral purposes, or, in other words, transformed it into the Fable proper. A collection of these seems to have existed previously and independently, in which the Fables were associated with the name of a mythical sage, Kasyâpa. These were appropriated by the early Buddhists by the simple expedient of making Kasyâpa the immediately preceding incarnation of the Buddha. A number of his *itihâsas* or Tales were included in the sacred Buddhistic work containing the "Jātakas" or previous-births of the Buddha, in some of which the Bodisat (or future Buddha) appears as one of the Dramatis Personae of the Fables; the Crane, *e.g.*, in our *Wolf and Crane* being one of the incarnations of the Buddha. So, too, the Lamb of our *Wolf and Lamb* was once Buddha; it was therefore easy for him—so the Buddhists thought—to remember and tell these Fables as incidents of his former careers. It is obvious that the whole idea of a Fable as an anecdote about a man masquerading in the form of a beast could most easily arise and gain currency where the theory of transmigration was vividly credited.

The Fables of Kasyâpa, or rather the moral verses (*gathas*) which served as a *memoria technica* to them, were probably carried over to Ceylon in 241 B.C. along with the Jātakas. About 300 years later (say 50 A.D.) some 100 of these were brought by a Cingalese embassy to Alexandria, where they were translated under the title of "Libyan Fables" (Λόγοι Λυβικοί), which had been earlier applied to similar stories that had percolated to Hellas from India; they were attributed to "Kybises." This collection seems to have introduced the habit of summing up the teaching of a Fable in the Moral, corresponding to the *gatha* of the Jātakas. About the end of the first century A.D. the Libyan Fables of "Kybises" became known to the Rabbinic school at Jabne, founded by R. Jochanan ben Saccai, and a number of the Fables translated into Aramaic which are still extant in the Talmud and Midrash.

In the Roman world the two collections of Demetrius and "Kybises" were brought together by Nicostratus, a rhetor attached to the court of Marcus

Aurelius. In the earlier part of the next century (c. 230 A.D.) this *corpus* of the ancient fable, Aesopic and Libyan, amounting in all to some 300 members, was done into Greek verse with Latin accentuation (choliambics) by Valerius Babrius, tutor to the young son of Alexander Severus. Still later, towards the end of the fourth century, forty-two of these, mainly of the Libyan section, were translated into Latin verse by one Avian, with whom the ancient history of the Fable ends.

In the Middle Ages it was naturally the Latin Phaedrus that represented the Aesopic Fable to the learned world, but Phaedrus in a fuller form than has descended to us in verse. A selection of some eighty fables was turned into indifferent prose in the ninth century, probably at the Schools of Charles the Great. This was attributed to a fictitious Romulus. Another prose collection by Ademar of Chabannes was made before 1030, and still preserves some of the lines of the lost Fables of Phaedrus. The Fables became especially popular among the Normans. A number of them occur on the Bayeux Tapestry, and in the twelfth century England, the head of the Angevin empire, became the home of the Fable, all the important adaptations and versions of Aesop being made in this country. One of these done into Latin verse by Walter the Englishman became the standard Aesop of medieval Christendom. The same history applies in large measure to the Fables of Avian, which were done into prose, transferred back into Latin verse, and sent forth through Europe from England.

Meanwhile Babrius had been suffering the same fate as Phaedrus. His scazons were turned into poor Greek prose, and selections of them pass to this day as the original Fables of Aesop. Some fifty of these were selected and, with the addition of a dozen Oriental fables, were attributed to an imaginary Persian sage, Syntipas; this collection was translated into Syriac, and thence into Arabic, where they passed under the name of the legendary Lôqman (probably a doublet of Balaam). A still larger collection of the Greek prose versions got into Arabic, where it was enriched by some sixty fables from the Arabic Bidpai and other sources, but still passed under the name of Aesop. This collection, containing 164 fables, was brought to England after the Third Crusade of Richard I, and translated into Latin by an Englishman named Alfred, with the aid of an Oxford Jew named Berachyah ha-Nakdan ("Benedictus le Puncteur" in the English Records), who, on his own account, translated a number of the fables into Hebrew rhymed prose, under the Talmudic title *Mishle Shu'alim* (Fox Fables). Part of Alfred's Aesop was translated into English alliterative verse, and this again was translated about 1200 into French by Marie de France, who attributed the new fables to King Alfred. After her no important addition was made to the medieval Aesop.

With the invention of printing the European book of Aesop was compiled about 1480 by Heinrich Stainhöwel, who put together the Romulus with selections from Avian, some of the Greek prose versions of Babrius from Ranuzio's translation, and a few from Alfred's Aesop. To these he added the legendary life of Aesop and a selection of somewhat loose tales from Petrus Alphonsi and Poggio Bracciolini, corresponding to the Milesian and Sybaritic tales which were associated with the Fable in antiquity. Stainhöwel translated all this into German, and within twenty years his collection had been turned into French, English (by Caxton, in 1484), Italian, Dutch, and Spanish. Additions were made to it by Brandt and Waldis in Germany, by L'Estrange in England, and by La Fontaine in France; these were chiefly from the larger Greek collections published after Stainhöwel's day, and, in the case of La Fontaine, from Bidpai and other Oriental sources. But these additions have rarely taken hold, and the Aesop of modern Europe is in large measure Stainhöwel's, even to the present day. The first three quarters of the present collection are Stainhöwel mainly in Stainhöwel's order. Selections from it passed into spelling and reading books, and made the Fables part of modern European folk-lore.[1]

We may conclude this history of Aesop with a similar account of the progress of Aesopic investigation. First came collection; the Greek Aesop was brought together by Neveletus in 1610, the Latin by Nilant in 1709. The main truth about the former was laid down by the master-hand of Bentley during a skirmish in the Battle of the Books; the equally great critic Lessing began to unravel the many knotty points connected with the medieval Latin Aesop. His investigations have been carried on and completed by three Frenchmen in the present century, Robert, Du Méril, and Hervieux; while three Germans, Crusius, Benfey, and Mall, have

---

[1] An episode in the history of the modern Aesop deserves record, if only to illustrate the law that Aesop always begins his career as a political weapon in a new home. When a selection of the Fables were translated into Chinese in 1840 they became favourite reading with the officials, till a high dignitary said, "This is clearly directed against *us*," and ordered Aesop to be included in the Chinese *Index Expurgatorius*.

thrown much needed light on Babrius, on the Oriental Aesop, and on Marie de France. Lastly, I have myself brought together these various lines of inquiry, and by adding a few threads of my own, have been able to weave them all for the first time into a consistent pattern.

So much for the past of the Fable. Has it a future as a mode of literary expression? Scarcely; its method is at once too simple and too roundabout. Too roundabout; for the truths we have to tell we prefer to speak out directly and not by way of allegory. And the truths the Fable has to teach are too simple to correspond to the facts of our complex civilisation; its rude *graffiti* of human nature cannot reproduce the subtle gradations of modern life. But as we all pass through in our lives the various stages of ancestral culture, there comes a time when these rough sketches of life have their appeal to us as they had for our forefathers. The allegory gives us a pleasing and not too strenuous stimulation of the intellectual powers; the lesson is not too complicated for childlike minds. Indeed, in their grotesque grace, in their quaint humour, in their trust in the simpler virtues, in their insight into the cruder vices, in their innocence of the fact of sex, Aesop's Fables are as little children. They are as little children, and for that reason they will forever find a home in the heaven of little children's souls.

An Afterword by

CLIFTON FADIMAN

"He killed the goose that laid the golden eggs."
"Yes, but who'll bell the cat?"
"He's a wolf in sheep's clothing."
"Fine feathers don't make fine birds."
"Sour grapes!"
"Don't be a dog in the manger."
"Don't count your chickens before they're hatched."

You may have heard people use these sayings, or you may have read them somewhere, or you may have said them yourself. They're so familiar that they seem to be part of the language. But, now that you've read this book, you know where they come from. (I didn't remember, for example, until I reread Aesop, that the saying about putting one's shoulder to the wheel goes back to "Hercules and the Wagoner," on page 98.)

Aesop was a Greek slave, or he might have come from Phrygia, an ancient country in Asia Minor. We don't really know much about him, but there is a tradition that he used to tell these fables in order to make his point in an argument. He almost surely didn't invent them himself, but his name got linked to them, and so for 2,500 years (Aesop may have died in 564 B.C.) we have been calling them the Fables of Aesop. The "morals" that appear at the end of most of the stories were probably tacked on long after Aesop's time, perhaps by some of the people who have retold the fables over the years. This version, by the great folklore scholar, Joseph Jacobs, is certainly one of the most charming.

It's easy to see what they are—really short lessons about how people behave, wrapped up in little stories. Most of them use animals as characters, and that makes them more vivid (and sometimes funnier) than if only human beings were in them.

Suppose I told you this story: "Jimmy's father offered him fifty cents to shovel away a heavy fall of snow in front of the house. At first Jimmy was discouraged. But he tackled the job, worked away slowly hour after hour, and little by little the snow was cleared away, and so he earned his fifty cents." That's just about as dull a story as you've ever heard, isn't it?

Now compare it with the fable on page 77, called "The Crow and the Pitcher." Which is better? Which will you remember longer?

Well, people have been enjoying these fables for thousands of years, partly because, though simple, they are quite wise and funny—and partly because they're about animals. I said they were simple. That's true, but some are cleverer than you might think at a first quick reading. Take, for example, "The Lion and the Statue," on page 50. That's pretty smart.

Some have a rather grim wisdom, like "The Eagle and the Arrow," on page 94. Others are just charming, like "The Old Woman and the Wine Jar," on page 95. (This is one of the few fables not about animals.)

It's interesting to compare fables with the fairy

stories you've read. Fairy stories are full of things that couldn't really happen, but that we wish *could* happen. What we enjoy is the story—and we don't mind its being "untrue." Fables, on the other hand, are down-to-earth, full of practicality, little mirrors reflecting ordinary human life, even though the characters are animals. Fairy tales make better reading, I think, but fables are shrewder, crammed with common sense. They make us feel that thousands of years ago human beings learned from daily living the same tough, practical lessons you and I have to learn today. *Familiarity breeds contempt* is just as true now as it was long ago when Aesop illustrated the statement through the actions of the Fox and the Lion.

About the author

AESOP

It is not known whether Aesop was an actual person,
a creation of popular legend, or even several people.
We believe that he lived during the sixth century B.C.
and was a Greek slave of deformed physique but
nimble wit, by which he earned his freedom. He is
said to have lived afterwards at the glittering court of
King Croesus and, on a mission for him to Delphi, to
have met his death at the hands of an angry mob.

About the adapter

JOSEPH JACOBS

JOSEPH JACOBS was born in Sydney, Australia, in 1854,
and was educated at St. John's College, Cambridge.
Primarily a scholar of Jewish history and affairs, he was
a prolific journalist, author, editor, and translator in
a variety of fields. His collections of folklore—partic-
ularly the volumes of English and Irish fairy tales—
set a standard for the selection and retelling of folk
material for children. He was living in Yonkers, New
York, at the time of his death in 1916.

About the artist

DAVID LEVINE

DAVID LEVINE was born in Brooklyn, New York, in 1926. He attended the Tyler School of Fine Arts in Philadelphia, Pennsylvania, and the Hans Hofmann School in New York City. Mr. Levine's work has been exhibited at many galleries and museums across the country, including the Corcoran Gallery in Washington, D.C., the Art Institute of Chicago, and Nebraska University Museum. He has had six one-man exhibitions at the Davis Galleries in New York City.

Mr. Levine's drawings appear in every issue of *The New York Review of Books*, and have been featured in *Horizon*, *Esquire*, and *McCall's*. He has won five awards, including the Tiffany Foundation Award, the Maynard Prize, and the Thomas B. Clarke Prize from the National Academy of Design. Mr. Levine has illustrated another Macmillan Classic, *Rip Van Winkle and the Legend of Sleepy Hollow*, and *The Heart of Stone*, a German fairy tale. He is presently teaching at the Brooklyn Museum Art School.

THE MACMILLAN CLASSICS · These handsome editions offer children, teen-agers, and parents a distinguished home library of fine reading.

DISTINCTIVE ILLUSTRATIONS · AFTERWORDS BY CLIFTON FADIMAN

LITTLE MEN
BY LOUISA MAY ALCOTT
ILLUSTRATED BY PAUL HOGARTH

LITTLE WOMEN
BY LOUISA MAY ALCOTT
ILLUSTRATED BY BETTY FRASER

ANDERSEN'S FAIRY TALES
BY HANS CHRISTIAN
ANDERSEN
ILLUSTRATED BY
LAWRENCE BEALL SMITH

EAST OF THE SUN AND WEST OF THE MOON AND OTHER TALES
Collected by P. C. ASBJORNSEN
and JORGEN E. MOE
ILLUSTRATED BY TOM VROMAN

PRIDE AND PREJUDICE
BY JANE AUSTEN
ILLUSTRATED BY
BERNARDA BRYSON

THE WIZARD OF OZ
BY L. FRANK BAUM
ILLUSTRATED BY W. W. DENSLOW

JANE EYRE
BY CHARLOTTE BRONTE
ILLUSTRATED BY ATI FORBERG

WUTHERING HEIGHTS
BY EMILY BRONTE
ILLUSTRATED BY
BERNARDA BRYSON

ALICE'S ADVENTURES IN WONDERLAND AND THROUGH THE LOOKING-GLASS
BY LEWIS CARROLL
ILLUSTRATED BY SIR JOHN TENNIEL

THE AENEID FOR BOYS AND GIRLS
Retold by ALFRED J. CHURCH
ILLUSTRATED BY EUGENE KARLIN

THE ILIAD AND THE ODYSSEY OF HOMER
Retold by ALFRED J. CHURCH
ILLUSTRATED BY EUGENE KARLIN

THE ADVENTURES OF PINOCCHIO
BY C. COLLODI
ILLUSTRATED BY NAIAD EINSEL

THE RED BADGE OF COURAGE
BY STEPHEN CRANE
ILLUSTRATED BY HERSCHEL LEVIT

ROBINSON CRUSOE
BY DANIEL DEFOE
ILLUSTRATED BY
FEDERICO CASTELLON

A CHRISTMAS CAROL
BY CHARLES DICKENS
ILLUSTRATED BY JOHN GROTH

DAVID COPPERFIELD
BY CHARLES DICKENS
ILLUSTRATED BY N. M. BODECKER

A TALE OF TWO CITIES
BY CHARLES DICKENS
ILLUSTRATED BY
RICHARD M. POWERS

TALES OF SHERLOCK HOLMES
BY SIR ARTHUR
CONAN DOYLE
ILLUSTRATED BY
HARVEY DINNERSTEIN

THE THREE MUSKETEERS
BY ALEXANDRE DUMAS
ILLUSTRATED BY
JAMES DAUGHERTY

GRIMMS' FAIRY TALES
BY THE BROTHERS GRIMM
ILLUSTRATED BY ARNOLD ROTH

RIP VAN WINKLE AND THE LEGEND OF SLEEPY HOLLOW
BY WASHINGTON IRVING
ILLUSTRATED BY DAVID LEVINE

THE FABLES OF AESOP
Retold by JOSEPH JACOBS
ILLUSTRATED BY DAVID LEVINE

THE JUNGLE BOOKS
BY RUDYARD KIPLING
ILLUSTRATED BY ROBERT SHORE

TALES FROM SHAKESPEARE
BY CHARLES AND MARY LAMB
ILLUSTRATED BY
RICHARD M. POWERS

THE CALL OF THE WILD
BY JACK LONDON
ILLUSTRATED BY KAREL KEZER

AT THE BACK OF THE NORTH WIND
BY GEORGE MacDONALD
ILLUSTRATED BY
HARVEY DINNERSTEIN

KING ARTHUR
Stories from Sir Thomas Malory's
Morte d'Arthur
Retold by MARY MacLEOD
ILLUSTRATED BY HERSCHEL LEVIT

MOBY DICK
BY HERMAN MELVILLE
ILLUSTRATED BY ROBERT SHORE

THE SCARLET PIMPERNEL
BY BARONESS ORCZY
ILLUSTRATED BY JOHN FALTER

TALES AND POEMS OF EDGAR ALLAN POE
ILLUSTRATED BY RUSSELL HOBAN

BLACK BEAUTY
BY ANNA SEWELL
ILLUSTRATED BY JOHN GROTH

FIVE LITTLE PEPPERS
BY MARGARET SIDNEY
ILLUSTRATED BY
ANNA MARIE MAGAGNA

HEIDI
BY JOHANNA SPYRI
ILLUSTRATED BY GRETA ELGAARD

ENGLISH FAIRY TALES
Retold by FLORA ANNIE STEEL
ILLUSTRATED BY
ARTHUR RACKHAM

TREASURE ISLAND
BY ROBERT LOUIS
STEVENSON
ILLUSTRATED BY JOHN FALTER

GULLIVER'S TRAVELS
BY JONATHAN SWIFT
Retold by PADRAIC COLUM
ILLUSTRATED BY WILLY POGANY

THE ADVENTURES OF HUCKLEBERRY FINN
BY MARK TWAIN
ILLUSTRATED BY JOHN FALTER

THE ADVENTURES OF TOM SAWYER
BY MARK TWAIN
ILLUSTRATED BY JOHN FALTER

TWENTY THOUSAND LEAGUES UNDER THE SEA
BY JULES VERNE
ILLUSTRATED BY CHARLES MOLINA

REBECCA OF SUNNYBROOK FARM
BY KATE DOUGLAS WIGGIN
ILLUSTRATED BY
LAWRENCE BEALL SMITH